THUNDERSTORM

Dedicated to my father, Leonard Geisert

www.enchantedlion.com

All of the illustrations in this book were produced from copperplate etchings that were first hand printed
and then hand colored using watercolor paints.

First American edition published in 2013 by Enchanted Lion Books, 20 Jay Street, M-18, Brooklyn, NY 11201

Library of Congress Control Number: 2012952191

ISBN 978-1-59270-133-9

Printed in November 2012 by South China Printing Company, China

THUNDERSTORM

ARTHUR GEISERT

ENCHANTED LION BOOKS · NEW YORK

SATURDAY AFTERNOON   JULY 15   12:15 PM

12:20 PM

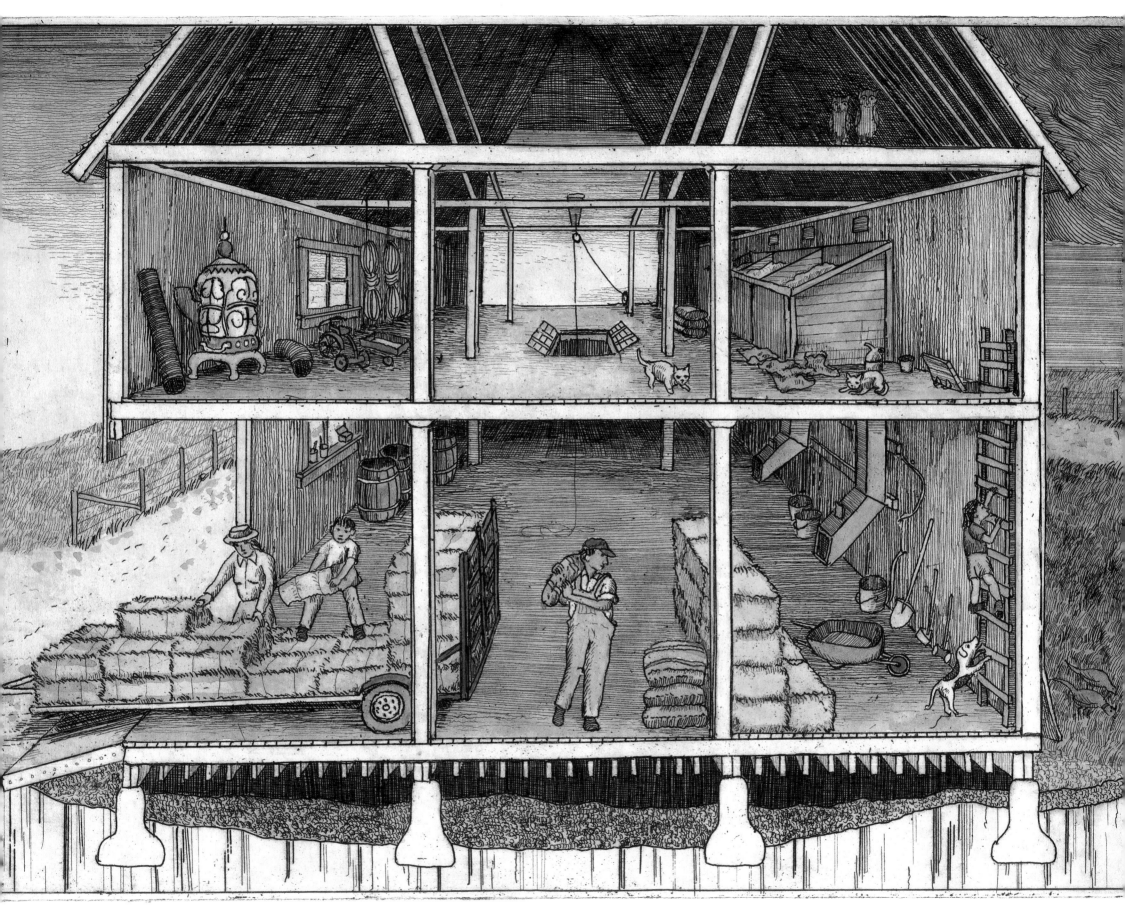

12:55 PM

1:08 PM

1:40 PM

2:25 PM

2:35 PM

2:50 PM

3:00 PM

3:45 PM

3:51 PM

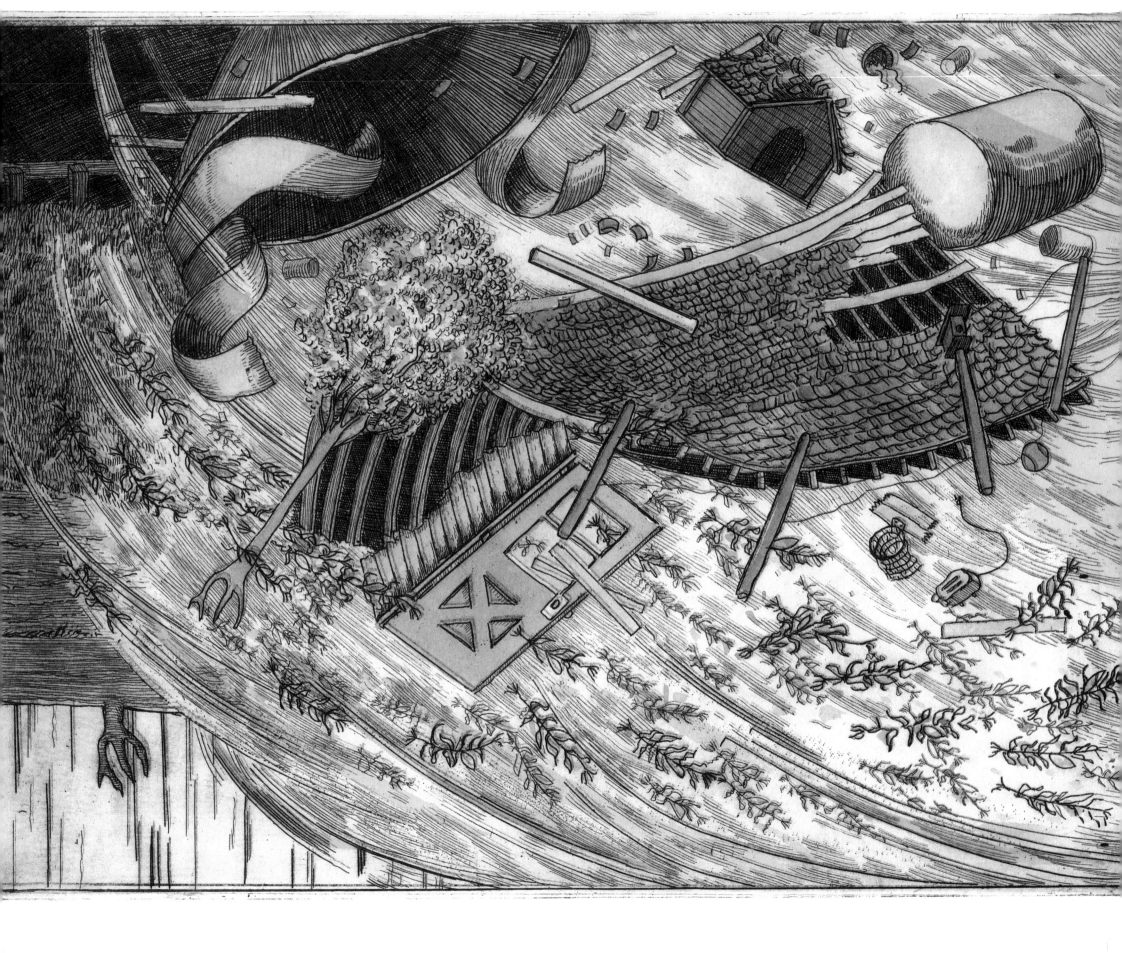

3:53 PM

4:30 PM

6:05 PM